# The HAIRY CANARIES
## and other Nonsense

By Martin Waddell

Illustrated by Alan Case

## Contents

LONGMAN

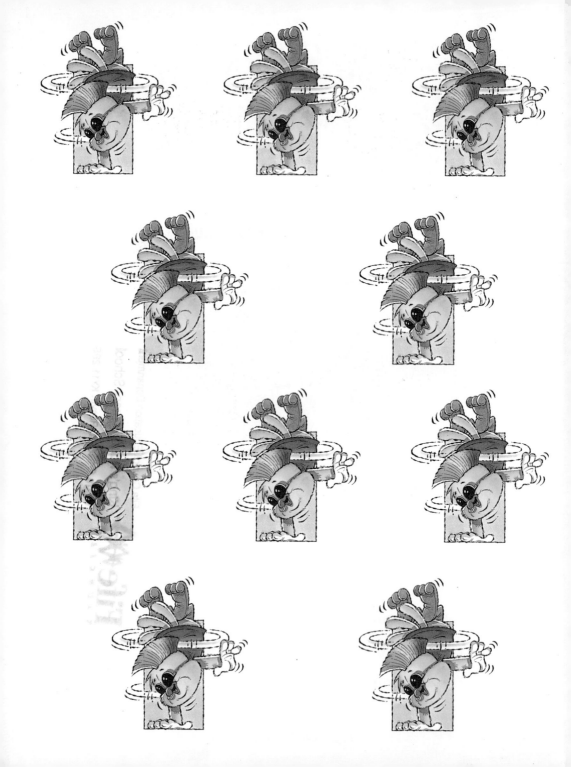

# The Hairy Canaries

Here come the Hairy Canaries.

Oscar and Chas and Boot and Winnie.

They are stars!

They don't chirp like other canaries.

They toot and whistle and twang and boom.

Oscar plays the trumpet. He's the hooter.

Chas plays the whistle.

Boot is on the guitar and

Winnie boom–booms on the drums.

They are the Hairy Canary Band.

Mr Bird looks after them.

He polishes the whistle and the trumpet,

tunes the guitar and packs the drum kit.

Then they have their birdseed, and they hit the road!

In the back of the big car, they do their hair.

Oscar has a ponytail.

Chas has long golden hair.

Boot is the Mohawk...

and Winnie's hair is gold, with blue sparklers in it.

They go on TV. All the other canaries love them.
There's a TV set in every birdcage, tuned to the
Hairy Canary Hour.
Nobirdy takes bird baths when they're on.
Nobirdy plays bells or pecks their plumes.
Everybirdy has a ball!

Here they come!

Toot! Peep! Bang! Boom!

All the canaries are doing their nuts!

Fanning their feathers!

Banging their beaks!

Pinging their perches!

Clapping their claws!

It is Hairy Canary Showtime!

Oscar tells jokes.

Chas sings solo.

Boot does a break dance...

and Winnie waltzes.

The show is over.

All the other canaries switch off. They go back to bell banging and bird bathing and

seed pecking, but the Hairy Canaries don't.

They are all washed out.

Mr Bird drives them home in the big car.

No toots, no peeps, no twangs and not a single boom.

They all get on one big perch and have their beauty sleep.

They dream dreams.

While the Hairy Canaries sleep, Mr Bird does all the work.

He polishes their seed tray.

He fills their golden baths.

He oils their swings.

And he sorts out all their music for the next show.

He answers all their letters, and files away the feathers that fans send them.

He does it because he loves them.

We love them too.

Everyone loves them for they are

**The Hairy Canaries!**

# Sadie the Baby
## The fastest pram-girl in the West

This is the story of Sadie the Baby,
the fastest pram-girl in the West.

Sadie lived with her Ma in a cabin
at Yellowstone Pass,
where she gurgled and sang in her pram
with her rattles slung low in her nappy.

15

Then one day, Big Ned came that way.

Big Ned and the wicked Ned Gang.

They rode into town and held up the bank.

For they hadn't heard of Sadie the Baby.

"Stand and deliver!" Big Ned cried.

He took all their silver and gold,

then he ran from the bank and leapt on his horse,

and he rode out of town with his gang,

a-firing his gun in the air

and...

...of course,

he woke up Sadie the baby!

That was his big mistake.

Bang! went the gun, and Sadie stirred.

Bang! Bang! went the gun, and Sadie sat up.

She cried for her rusk.

She was teething.

Bang! Bang! Bang! went the gun,
as the Ned Gang rode on
in a big cloud of dust
that went over Sadie the Baby.

"My baby!" cried Ma,

running out to the pram.

"Fetch me my hoss!" muttered Sadie.

And her ma did.

(She knew not to say 'no' to Sadie the Baby.)

Far away on the prairie
the Ned Gang galloped,
pursued by a small cloud of dust and in it ...
... was Sadie the Baby.

The horse was hitched up to the front of the pram.
Sadie the Baby was urging it on with her rattle.

A mile, two miles,
three miles or more,
Sadie got faster as the bad men got slower
and then ...

"Stop in the name of The Baby!" cried Sadie,
who'd galloped ahead
to the end of the pass.
It was a Sadie the Baby ambush!

"Not for a baby!" cried Ned,
raising his gun,
but he was outdone
by a swiftly-flung teddy from out of the pram.

Rusk followed rusk
from the pram,
a hail of swift firing
a-driving the Ned Gang
out of their minds and then ...

Sadie charged with her rattle among them,
skilfully swinging her pram,
knocking their hats off and
squirting her bottle right in their eyes.

They'd had enough,
had the evil Ned Gang,
and they all ran away,
except for Big Ned
who was pinned to the ground,
knocked on the head by a Ted,
a Ted that belonged to our Sadie!

Sadie rode home in her pram
with Big Ned trussed up in a spare nappy behind her.
The sheriff cried, "Sadie, you've done it again!"
"It was nothing much, pardner!" said Sadie.

That was the end of Big Ned and his gang,

another notch on her rattle for Sadie.

But it just goes to show

if you go to the West

don't tangle with Sadie the Baby.

My Dinosaur Days

By Rover

Once upon a long time ago in the dinosaur days,
there was a tiny Brontosaurus named Betty
who lived in a cave with her mum and her dad
and her little petman.
His name was Benedict, but she called him 'Rover'.

Every day when the sun rose,

Betty took Rover for his walk.

She let him off the lead in the park.

Betty threw trees for him,

and patted his head when he brought them back,

and gave him fresh cabbage to eat as a treat,

when he was good.

Rover was always very good,

because Betty was kind to him

but after a bit,

he began to go off his cabbage.

When Betty threw his tree

Rover just sat there and looked stupid,

wagging his bottom.

"Go on Rover. Fetch!" Betty said,

but Rover wouldn't.

Betty got very cross.
She jumped up and down banging her tail,
so that the mountains shook
and the earth vibrated.
Rover got scared and ran away.
"Come back Rover!" Betty called,
and she ran after him.

Rover had run right into the Primeval Forest,

where he hid under leaves of Guzzle-um Tree.

Betty was a bit short sighted so she

waddled right past him,

knocking down trees as she went and,

now and then,

eating one when she felt peckish.

'Hey-ho!' thought Rover,

who was fed up with walking about attached to a lead.

'Now for a little adventure!'

And he went off to have one,

which was silly,

because you never know what you'll meet

in the Primeval Forest.

The first thing he met was a Wooooooo.
It had never seen a man before,
but a man looked more or less
like walking breakfast,
so he tried to take a nip.
Rover only just got away,
by swinging through the branches.

That was a mistake,
because up in the sky
was a Boooooooooooooooo
who thought he looked like a
tasty snack
so it flew down from the sky
and dive boomed him
but Rover got away,
by jumping in the lake.

Snap! Snap! Snap!
Snappity-Snappity-Snap –
the lake was full of
Krooooooooooooos
who looked like lumps of mud
but snapped with great big shiny teeth.
Rover only just made it out of the lake
with his bear skin intact.

"Oh-oh-oh-oh-oh!" Rover lay panting on the bank
and then
Scrunch-crash-bang-smash,
something came at him through the woods.
Poor Rover!
He was too tired to escape any more
but...

"Rover! Rover!" called the something
and it whistled Rover's whistle.
It was Betty!
With one bound Rover was up on her lap,
wagging his bottom and eating his cabbage.

"Don't you ever run away on me again, Rover!" Betty said,
and she put him on the lead.
She took Rover home
and she tucked him up
in his kennel.

Rover never ran away again.

Instead, he wrote down all his adventures

on the wall of the cave

and years later

someone found them

which is how

this tale

came to be told.

# The Clock in the Hall

This is the story
Of Mrs McMinn
Who locked herself out
And locked her clock in.

She'd hidden the door key
Under her hat
But she had forgotten
To remember that.
So...

She started to shout
And she started to bawl
But the clock in the hall said
Nothing at all!

43

She searched round the doorstep
And under the mat.
She emptied her handbag
All over the cat.
She dug up the garden
And crawled on her knees.
She found lots of mud
But she didn't find keys.

She started to shout
And she started to bawl
But the clock in the hall said
Nothing at all!

She went to her tree
Which she used as a ladder
And slowly climbed up it
Getting higher, but sadder.

She got to her window
But it wouldn't open
So she sat on the tree branch
Mud covered and mopin'.
Then...

She started to shout
And she started to bawl
But the clock in the hall said
Nothing at all!

The clock hands crept round
To one minute to three
But fat Mrs McMinn
Didn't know it, you see.

She sat on her branch
With the rain pouring down
Wishing she'd never
Gone into town.
Then...

The clock in the hall
Struck one, two and three
And surprised the fat lady
Who fell out of her tree!

She fell splash in the mud
And flattened the cat
And the key of the door
Fell out of her hat!

When she let herself in
And made herself tea
She said, "Thank you, dear clock,
For rescuing me."

She didn't shout,
She didn't bawl,
And the clock in the hall said
"'Twas nothing at all!"

# The Hat House

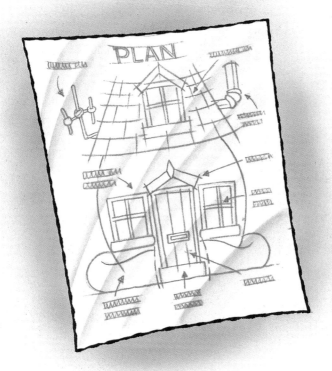

One day Fred and Maurice met in the park.

Fred is the one with the bird on his head, and Maurice has the green hat.

"Pardon me, Fred," said Maurice. "But there's a bird on your head."

"Stupid bird thinks I'm a tree," said Fred.

The bird didn't say anything.

"Silly bird!" said Maurice.

Fred was very upset.

He was fed up being taken for a tree, and getting feathers in his ears.

"I wish I was small!" he said.

Fred started to shrink.

Only a bit at first, until his bird got into a panic and flew off.

It had never nested on a shrinking tree before.

"Hi up there!" shouted Maurice. "What are you doing?"

"I'm on my way down," said Fred, happily.

And he was.

Down and down and down and down.

"Hold on a bit," said Maurice. "You're about the right size now."

"Can't stop!" gasped Fred.

Down and down and down and down.

"Stopped!" said Fred, smiling at Maurice.

"Only just in time!" said Maurice.

"This is nice," said Fred but...

Down...

down...

and on down...

he went,

slowly,

because

the

wish

was

wearing

off.

"Where are you Fred?" asked Maurice.

"Here!" said Fred.

"Where's here?" said Maurice.

"Sitting on this dandelion," said Fred.

"Which dandelion?" said Maurice.

"The small one," said Fred.

The bird flew down and took a look at him, and
then it flew away. Birds don't perch on dandelions.
"Like it down there, Fred?" said Maurice.
"No!" said Fred.
"Why not?" said Maurice.
"Worried about spiders and ladybirds," said Fred.
"Wish yourself up a bit," Maurice suggested.

Fred tried, but nothing happened.

"Looks like I'm stuck on this dandelion," he said.

"No you're not," said Maurice, and he picked Fred up and put him in his top pocket, beside the pens.

"Careful does it," said Fred, hanging on to a ball point.

"All right now, Fred?" asked Maurice.

"Not really, Maurice," said Fred. "I'm not comfy in this pocket."

"Good view from there, I expect?" said Maurice.

"If you like that sort of thing," said Fred, who didn't.

"I've got a very cosy inside pocket," suggested Maurice.

"Too dark," said Fred.

"Beggars can't be choosers, Fred," said Maurice.

"I'm not a beggar, Maurice," said Fred. "I'm just rather unexpectedly small."

"Suit yourself then!" said Maurice.

And Fred started moping.

"Why are you moping, Fred?" asked Maurice.

"I'm not a top pocket type person, Maurice," said Fred.

"I don't want to spend the rest of my days in a row of pens."

So Maurice moved the pens in his top pocket, which gave Fred a little more room, but not much.

"How's that?" he said.

"Rotten!" said Fred.

Then Maurice had an idea.

This is it:

"BRILLIANT!" said Fred, when he saw the plans.

They went home to Maurice's house, and Maurice set to work.

He did the big bits.

And Fred did the fiddly bits.

This is Fred's house, finished.

And this is Fred in it.

"All right up there, Fred?" said Maurice.

"Perfectly thank you, Maurice," said Fred.

"Happy?" said Maurice.

"Very," said Fred.

He was, and they were.

They are still.

You'll know them if you see them.

Maurice is the one with the house in his hat.

Fred is the one who lives there.

The bird is back up in the tree.

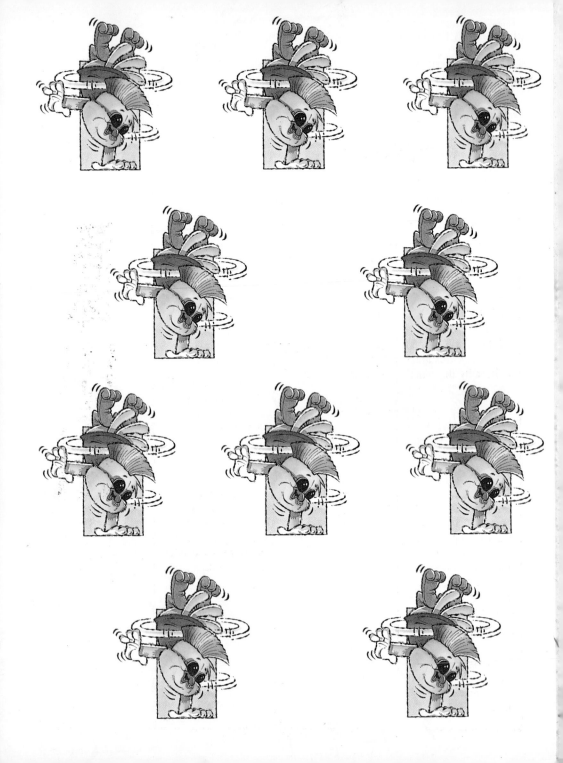